Room One,
First-Grade Friends

Mr. Scary

Junie B. Jones

Tattletale May

Herb

Lennie

José

Sheldon

Shirley

Lucille

Roger

Camille

Chenille

Laugh Out Loud with Junie B. Jones!

junie b. jones®
First Grader
(at last!)

by BARBARA PARK

illustrated by
Denise Brunkus

A STEPPING STONE BOOK™

Random House 🏠 New York

To my "almost" sisters,
Kathy Kiefer and Marlene Day.
You're simply the best.

Text copyright © 2001 by Barbara Park
Cover art and interior illustrations copyright © 2001 by Denise Brunkus

All rights reserved. Published in the United States by
Random House Children's Books, a division of Random House LLC,
a Penguin Random House Company, New York.

Random House and the colophon are registered trademarks and A Stepping
Stone Book and the colophon are trademarks of Random House LLC.
Junie B. Jones is a registered trademark of Barbara Park, used under license.

JunieBJones.com

Educators and librarians, for a variety of teaching tools, visit us at
RHTeachersLibrarians.com

This title was originally cataloged by the Library of Congress as follows:
Park, Barbara.
Junie B., first grader (at last!) / by Barbara Park ; illustrated by Denise Brunkus.
    p. cm. (Junie B. Jones series ; #18)
Summary: Junie B. thinks first grade is a flop when her kindergarten friend Lucille
prefers the company of twins Camille and Chenille and Junie B. needs glasses.
ISBN 978-0-375-80293-5 (trade) — ISBN 978-0-375-90293-2 (lib. bdg.)
ISBN 978-0-375-81516-4 (pbk.) — ISBN 978-0-375-89442-8 (ebook)
[1. Schools—Fiction. 2. Eyeglasses—Fiction. 3. Friendship—Fiction.]
I. Brunkus, Denise, ill. II. Title.
III. Series: Park, Barbara. Junie B. Jones series ; 18.
PZ7.P2197 Jtwg 2001 [Fic]—dc21 2001019076

Printed in the United States of America 45 44 43 42

This book has been officially leveled by using the F&P Text Level Gradient™
Leveling System.

Contents

1

First-Grade Surprises

Thursday

Dear first-grade journal,

Yesterday was the first day
of school. It is new here.

Today my teacher handed
out these journals. He is
making us write in these dumb
things. Only I don't even know
what to write.

My teacher has muscles and

mustache

a ~~mustash~~.

His name is Mr. Scary.

He made that name up, I believe.

I am not even scared of him, hardly.

From,

Junie B., First Grader

I put down my pencil. And I looked at what I wrote.

I did a sigh.

"I would like to go home now," I said to just myself.

"Shh!" said a girl named May. "I'm still trying to do my work."

May sits next to me in the back of the room.

I do not actually care for that girl.

Just then, my teacher stood up at his desk. His mustache smiled real friendly.

"Okay, boys and girls. You can stop writing now," he said. "As I told you earlier, we will be working in our journals quite often this year. In fact, it won't be long until your journal starts feeling like an old friend."

I rolled my eyes at the ceiling.

"What kind of an old friend looks like a dumb notebook?" I said.

"Shh!" said May again. "You shouldn't talk while the teacher is talking, Junie Jones!"

I looked at her real annoyed.

"*B.*," I said. "My name is Junie *B.* I

think I have mentioned that to you before, May."

I leaned closer to her face.

"B., B., B., B., B.," I said.

After that, I slumped in my seat. And I put my head on my desk.

I peeked at the other children who sit near me.

Their names are Herb. And Lennie. And José.

I do not know them from a hole in the ground.

I did another sigh.

First grade is not what it's cracked up to be.

My room is named Room One.

I was nervous when I came here yesterday.

That's how come Daddy had to carry me all the way to the room. 'Cause my legs felt like squishy Jell-O.

He put me down outside the door.

"Well, here we are, Junie B.," he said. "*First* grade. At *last*."

My stomach had flutterflies in it.

Also, my arms had prickly goose bumps. And my forehead had drops of sweaty.

"I am a wreck," I said.

Daddy smiled very nice.

"There's nothing to worry about, Junie B. I promise," he said. "You're going to *love* first grade. Just think. There's a whole roomful of brand-new friends just waiting to meet you."

He ruffled my hair. "Are you ready to go in now?" he asked. "Hmm? Are you ready to begin your first-grade adventure?"

I looked at him a real long time.

Then I quick spun around. And I zoomed down the hall as fast as I could!

Daddy zoomed after me!

He caught up with me speedy quick. And he carried me back to my class.

Only this time, he carried me straight into the room!

As soon as he put me down again, I hid behind his legs.

'Cause that place was a zoo, I tell you!

There were people *everywhere*! There were girls and boys. And mothers and daddies. And grandmas and grampas. Plus also, there were drooly babies in strollers.

Then, all of a sudden, my whole mouth came open!

Because good news! I finally saw someone I knew!

I jumped up and down and all around.

"DADDY! DADDY! IT'S LUCILLE!" I hollered. "REMEMBER LUCILLE? LUCILLE WAS MY BESTEST FRIEND FROM KINDERGARTEN LAST YEAR!"

Lucille was standing at a desk next to the window.

I ran to her in a jiffy.

Then I hugged and hugged that girl! And I couldn't even stop!

"LUCILLE! LUCILLE! IT'S ME! IT'S ME! IT'S YOUR BESTEST FRIEND FROM KINDERGARTEN . . . JUNIE B. JONES!"

I tried to pick her up.

"I AM SO GLAD TO SEE YOU, FRIEND!" I shouted real joyful.

Lucille pulled my arms off her.

"Stop it, Junie B.! Stop it!" she said.

"You're wrinkling my new back-to-school dress! This thing cost a fortune."

I stopped hugging her.

Lucille smoothed and fluffed herself.

I smoothed and fluffed her, too.

"There," I said. "Good as new."

After that, I grabbed Lucille's hand. And I started to pull.

"Come on, Lucille. Let's go find two desks together," I said. "I think we should sit near the door. Want to? Huh? If we sit near the door, we can stare at people who walk down the hall."

Lucille yanked her hand away.

"*No*, Junie B. No. I'm going to sit at this desk right here," she said. "I already picked it out with my two new friends, Camille and Chenille."

She pointed at the door.

"See them over there?" she said. "I met them before you came. They are saying good-bye to their mother. Aren't they precious?"

I looked at Camille and Chenille.

And guess what?

My eyes popped right out of my head!

Because wowie wow wow!

Those girls were *twins*, that's why!

I sprang way high in the air.

"TWINS! TWINS! THEY'RE TWINS,
LUCILLE! THIS IS OUR LUCKY DAY!"

I pulled on her again.

"Come on, Lucille! Let's go touch them!

Hurry! Hurry! Before a line forms!"

Lucille did not budge a muscle.

"Stop it, Junie B.! Quit pulling on me," she said. "Camille and Chenille don't want to be touched. And besides, *I* am their new best friend. Not *you*."

I looked surprised at that girl.

"Yes, but I can be their bestest friend along with you. Right, Lucille?" I asked. "All I have to do is meet them, right? And then all of us can be bestest friends together."

Lucille shook her head.

"No, Junie B. I'm sorry. But you and I have already *been* best friends, remember?" she said. "We were best friends for a whole long year. And so now it's time for Camille and Chenille to get a turn."

She did a shrug. "It's only fair of me,"

she said. "And besides, their names *rhyme* with my name. And yours doesn't."

She wrinkled her nose very cute. "*Camille* and *Chenille* and *Lucille*. See? Isn't that darling?"

After that, Lucille gave me a pat.

"Don't be sad, okay?" she said. "You and I can still be friends, Junie B. Just not on a regular basis."

After that, she waved her fingers.

And she said *ta-ta*.

And she skipped to Camille and Chenille.

2
More Surprises . . .
Plus Herb

Mother and Daddy keep trying to cheer me up about first grade.

Mother says sometimes life has disappointments in it.

Daddy says sometimes you have to roll with the punches.

I say first grade is a flop.

Last year, I had two bestest friends.

First, I had Lucille.

Plus also, I had that Grace.

Me and that Grace rode the school bus together every single day.

Only too bad for us. Because this year, Grace got put in a different room than me. And that was not even fair.

But hurray, hurray! Me and Grace still decided to ride the bus together! Because that's what friendship is for, I think.

And so last week, both of us sat next to each other . . . just like we always did!

Only, what do you know?

On Monday morning, Grace got on the bus with a *new* girl from her class. And those two plopped down in the seat right in front of me!

I quick jumped up. And I tapped on Grace's head.

"Grace?" I said. "*Excuse* me. Grace? What kind of shenanigans do you call this,

madam? Didn't you see me sitting here?"

Grace waved at me real friendly.

"Yes. Hi, Junie B.," she said. "I'm sorry I can't sit with you today. But I promised Bobbi Jean Piper I would sit with her this morning. Okay?"

I stamped my foot.

"No, Grace. *Not* okay. You can't sit with Bobbi Jean Piper," I said. "You and I have to sit together every single day. 'Cause we sat together every day last year. And this year shalt be no different."

Just then, Mr. Woo, the bus driver, closed the bus door.

He looked in his mirror at me.

"Sit down, please, Junie B.," he said.

Bobbi Jean Piper pointed and grinned.

"You got *yelled* at," she said kind of mean.

I made a scary face at that girl.

"Grr!" I said. *"Grr,* Bobbi Jean Piper."

Behind me, I heard a loud laugh.

I quick spun around.

And guess what?

It was Herb who sits in front of me in Room One!

"*Herb!*" I said real surprised. "I didn't even know that you rode this bus!"

Herb kept on laughing.

"You said *grr!*" he laughed. "*Grr!* Ha! That's a good one!"

I wrinkled my eyebrows at that boy.

"Yeah, only here's the problem, Herbert," I said. "*Grr* is not actually a joking matter. Plus, I wasn't even talking to you."

Herb quit laughing.

"I *know* you weren't talking to me," he said. "No one on this bus ever talks to me. That's because last year I went to a different school. So I don't have any bus friends yet."

Just then, the bus stopped at the next corner.

Herb came around the seat and sat next to me.

"Maybe, just for today, I can sit here,"

Then I did a big breath. And I looked at
Herb.

"Today is not off to a good start," I said
kind of quiet.

Herb nodded. "I hear you," he said.

I slumped way down in my seat.

"My bestest friends are dropping like flies," I said.

Herb nodded. "Join the club," he said.

"First grade is a flop," I said.

Herb nodded. "Totally," he said.

I looked out the window.

"*Grr,*" I said.

"*Grr,*" said Herb.

I smiled to just myself.

I think I might like this Herb.

3
Stumped

Me and Herb walked to Room One from the bus.

He waved to Mr. Scary.

Then I waved, too.

"I am not even scared of that teacher, hardly," I said to just myself.

We kept on walking to our seats.

May was already sitting at her desk. She was organizing her pencil box.

Lennie was at his desk, too.

Only wait till you hear this.

I didn't even recognize that guy, almost!

Because Lennie had a thrilling new haircut, that's why!

It was pointish and spikish and stiffish and straightish.

That hair can puncture you, I think.

"Whoa!" I said.

"Cool!" said Herb.

"*Gel,*" said Lennie.

"Shh!" said May.

Just then, José came hurrying down the row. He was rushing real fast. 'Cause the bell was almost ready to ring.

"Hola, everyone," he said, out of breath. "Hola, hola."

Me and Herb and Lennie looked curious at him.

José grinned.

"Whoops," he said. "*Hola* means *hello* in Spanish. I know two different languages,

and sometimes I forget which one I'm speaking."

"Wow, José!" I said. "You really speak two languages?"

"Cool," said Herb.

"Big deal," said May. "I know Spanish,

too. I can count all the way to three in Spanish. Does anyone want to hear me?"

The rest of us looked at each other.

"Not really," said Herb.

"Not me," said Lennie.

"Me neither," said José.

May didn't pay attention to us. "Uno, dos, tres," she said real loud.

I leaned nearer to her.

"Shh!" I said.

Then everyone laughed and laughed.

But not May.

Pretty soon, the bell rang for school.

Mr. Scary got our morning started.

First, he took attendance of the children. Then we said, *I pledge allegiance to the flag.* Plus also, we listened to boring bulletins from the office.

Finally, Mr. Scary walked to the chalkboard. And he printed a list of words.

"Boys and girls," he said. "This morning, I have a fun assignment for you."

He winked at us and pointed to the list.

"I want you to read these words to yourselves," he said. "Then—without talking to your neighbor—choose any word from the list and draw a picture of it in your journal."

May squealed very thrilled.

"Oh, goody, goody!" she said. "I love this kind of assignment, Mr. Scary. I am perfect at not talking to my neighbor!"

After that, she quick took a pencil out of her box. And she started to draw.

I stared at the words.

Then I tapped on my chin. And I scratched my head.

'Cause I didn't actually *get* this assignment, that's why.

"Hmm," I said. "Hmm. Hmm. Hmm."

I glanced my eyes at Herb and Lennie and José.

All of them were drawing, too.

I looked back at the board again.

Then I stretched my neck as far as it could go. And I squinted my hardest.

But those words had me stumped, I tell you!

Finally, I reached out to Herb real secret. And I tapped on his back.

"Psst. Herb," I whispered. "Quick question. Which word are you drawing?"

May did a loud gasp.

She jumped up from her seat and pointed at me.

"Mr. Scary! Mr. Scary! Junie Jones is talking to her neighbor! See her? She's talking to Herbert. And that is against the rules!"

I turned my head.

"Blabber-lips!" I yelled. "Blabber-lips May."

Mr. Scary looked back at us.

His mustache was not smiling.
I did a gulp.
Then I quick opened my journal.
And I started to draw.

4

Clucks

We drew and drew in our journals.

Mr. Scary waited until all of us were done.

Then he walked around the room. And he looked at everyone's pictures.

He gave out shiny gold stars.

First, he gave stars to Camille and Chenille.

"What great-looking dogs you drew, girls," he said. "Look at those floppy ears."

Lucille raised her hand.

"Look at mine, Teacher!" she said. "I

drew a cat with *pointy* ears. See? My rich nanna has an expensive cat just like this. Its fur is a foot thick, almost."

Mr. Scary looked strange at her.

"Really, Lucille? A whole foot of fur?" he said. "My, my."

He gave her a gold star and moved on.

He went to a boy named Roger. Roger was in my same class last year.

"*Excellent* job, Roger," Mr. Scary said. "You drew a man wearing a coat. The words *man* and *coat* were both on the board, weren't they?"

I did a little frown.

'Cause none of these words were actually sounding familiar.

After that, Mr. Scary walked to Sheldon and Shirley.

"Cool bat and ball, Sheldon," he said.

"And, Shirley! You drew a bat and ball, too, didn't you?"

I put my head on my desk.

Something was very wrong here.

Finally, Mr. Scary got to May.

"Oh, May," he said. "What a special clock you drew. The big hand has five fingers. That's very unusual."

"Yes," said May. "I created it myself. Plus, *clock* was the hardest word up there, wasn't it, Mr. Scary? I am the only one who even knew the word *clock*, I bet."

Just then, my stomach felt sickish inside.

I quick closed my journal and stuffed it in my desk.

Mr. Scary saw me.

"Junie B.?" he said. "Don't you want to show me your drawing? Don't you want a gold star for today?"

I shook my head real fast.

"Nope. No, thank you. No, I don't," I said. "Not today. I really, really don't care for a gold star today. But thank you for asking."

Mr. Scary kept on standing there.

"The end," I said.

He did not budge.

"Please move along," I said.

Finally, Mr. Scary bent down next to me.

He lowered his voice so no one could hear.

"I'm sorry, Junie B. But I'd really like to see what you drew," he said. "I need to make sure that you understood the assignment."

Then—before I knew it—he took my journal out of my desk. And he gave it to me to hold.

After that, he walked me into the hall. And he let me show him my drawing in private.

And guess what?

He liked it, I think!

"Oh, wow. Look at *that*, Junie B.," he said. "You drew a wonderful picture of a . . . a . . ."

He kept on looking. "A . . . a . . ."

"A screaming chicken," I said finally.

Mr. Scary did a strange face.

"Yes. *Right*," he said. "It's a . . ."

"Screaming chicken," I said again.

I pointed at the chicken's mouth.

"See how it's screaming, 'CLUCK! CLUCK! CLUCK!'? I used capital letters for the clucks. Capitals are for screaming. Correct?"

"Well, yes. I *suppose* so," said Mr. Scary.

"But—the thing is, Junie B.—the word *cluck* wasn't on the board today."

"I know it," I said. "The word on the board was *clock*. Only I didn't read all the letters right, I guess. 'Cause I accidentally thought it was *cluck*."

I tapped on my chin.

"What I actually wanted to draw was the *but and bull*," I said. "I really liked the sound of that one. But I didn't know how to get started, exactly. So I went ahead with the *cluck* idea."

Mr. Scary looked confused at me.

"The *but and bull*?" he asked.

I smiled kind of embarrassed.

"Yeah . . . well, I read those words wrong, too, I guess," I said. "They turned out to be *bat and ball*."

Mr. Scary frowned.

"Hmm," he said. "What about the other words on the board, Junie B.? Do you remember how you read some of the other ones? How about *dog* and *cat*? Or *coat* and *goat*?"

I thought back. Then I made my voice real quiet.

"*Dug* and *cot* and *coot* and *yoot*," I said.

Mr. Scary nodded his head.

Then he patted my hand very nice.

And he gave me back my journal.

And we walked back into Room One.

5
Bug Bag

Tuesday

Dear first-grade journal,

  Mr. Scary just called me in
from recess. All the other
children are still playing out
there.

  He said for me to write
in my journal for a minute and
he will be with me soon.

  I keep peeking at him from

behind these pages.

   He is printing sentences on the board. It is extra work for me, I think.

   I do not actually approve of this.

   From,
   Junie B., First Grader

Mr. Scary put down his chalk.

"You can stop peeking at me now, Junie B.," he said.

I looked at him real surprised. 'Cause that guy has eyes in the back of his hair, apparently.

He turned around and smiled.

"Do you see these three sentences that

I just wrote up here?" he asked.

"Yes," I said. "I see them."

"Excellent," said Mr. Scary. "Could you stand up and try reading them from back there, please?"

Just then, my heart got pumpy and pounding inside.

'Cause I'm not good at reading from the board, that's why.

I kept on sitting there.

"Please," said Mr. Scary. "Just give it a try, okay?"

Finally, I stood up. And I squinted at the sentences.

I read real slow.

"Bob . . . is . . . a . . . bug . . . bag," I read.

I did a teensy frown at that news.

"Really?" I asked. "Bob is a bug bag?"

Mr. Scary pointed to sentence number two. "Try this one," he said.

I squinted some more.

"I . . . like . . . my . . . hog . . . spit," I read again.

I looked at my teacher very curious.

"These sentences are oddballs, aren't they?" I said.

Mr. Scary pointed at the last one. "Just one more to go," he said.

This time, I stretched my neck. And I strained my eyes.

"Jack . . . is . . . going . . . to . . . to . . ."

I scrunched my eyes even smaller.

". . . to *jail*," I read.

I did a gasp.

"Really? No fooling? Jack who?"

Mr. Scary came back to my seat.

He took my hand and walked me closer to the board.

"Could you try reading them again from here, Junie B.?" he said.

I made my voice real whiny.

"But I don't *want* to read them again, Mr. Scary," I told him. "I already know what they say."

"Just one more time," he said.

And so finally, I did a big breath. And I read the sentences all in a row.

"Bob is a big boy."

"I like my dog, Spot."

"Jack is going to Jill's."

I covered my mouth very surprised.

"Hey! What do you know? He's going

to *Jill's,* Mr. Scary!" I said. "Whew! That's a relief, right?"

Mr. Scary laughed. "Right," he said.

After that, I headed for the door.

"Okey-doke. Well, I guess I'll be getting back to recess now," I said. "See ya."

I waited for him to answer.

He did not say *see ya.*

I turned around.

"See ya?" I said a little bit softer.

But Mr. Scary just shook his head no.

'Cause too bad for me.

He had other plans.

Mr. Scary took my hand.

We walked out of Room One and down the hall.

"You and I are going to visit Mrs. Weller, Junie B.," he said. "You remember

Mrs. Weller from last year, don't you?"

I shook my head no. 'Cause that name did not ring a bell.

"Mostly I would just like to remember recess," I said.

Mr. Scary patted my shoulder.

"Mrs. Weller is a lovely person," he said.

"Recess is a lovely person, too," I said.

"Mrs. Weller is the school nurse," he said.

I quick stopped walking.

Because the school nurse is where you go when you are sick or tired. And I was totally fine.

"But I am in good shape," I said. "See me? I don't even need a Band-Aid."

Mr. Scary smiled.

He pulled me along again.

"Of course you're in good shape, Junie

B.," he said. "But Mrs. Weller does lots of nice things besides giving out Band-Aids."

Just then, we walked into Mrs. Weller's office.

And guess what? I remembered her perfectly well! I just never knew she had a name before!

"Why, Junie B. Jones," she said. "What a nice surprise to see you again."

"It's a surprise to see you, too," I said. "'Cause I'm not even sick or tired. Plus also, I'm supposed to be on the playground right now."

Mrs. Weller laughed out loud. Only I don't actually know why.

After that, she and Mr. Scary whispered real quiet to each other.

Then finally, Mr. Scary patted my shoulder.

"I'm going to leave you with Mrs.
Weller for a while, Junie B.," he said. "The
two of you are going to play a game with
her eye chart. Okay?"

All of a sudden, my stomach felt kind of jumpy.

'Cause playing a game with the nurse did not sound fun.

No, I said inside my head. *Not okay.*

Mr. Scary waved.

"See you," he said.

I watched him go.

I did not say *see you* back.

6

The E Game

I sat in a chair next to Mrs. Weller's desk.

She asked me lots of questions.

First, she asked me how I liked my summer vacation. Then she asked me how I liked first grade. And how I liked Mr. Scary.

That is called stall talk, I believe.

Finally, Mrs. Weller stood up.

"Have you noticed the eye charts I have hanging on my wall, Junie B.?" she asked.

She pointed at them.

"Eye charts are posters that help us test our eyesight," she explained. "I have two

different kinds. See? One has alphabet letters on it. And the one right next to it is
filled with funny *E*'s. That one is called an
E chart."

I looked at that funny thing.

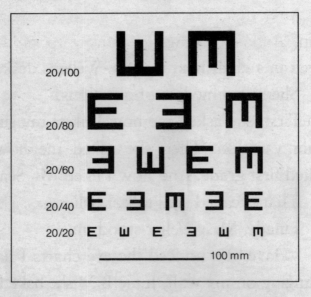

"Whoa," I said. "Those are the craziest
E's I ever saw. They are backwards and for-
wards and upside down."

"You're right," said Mrs. Weller. "The *E*'s are all mixed up, aren't they? And today you and I are going to play a game with those mixed-up *E*'s. It's called the E game."

After that, Mrs. Weller got a little paper cup. And she showed me how to hold it over one of my eyes.

"We're going to be testing each of your eyes separately," she said. "While one eye is hiding under the cup, the other eye will play the game. Okay?"

I shrugged my shoulders. 'Cause what choice did I have?

Mrs. Weller showed me where to stand to play the game. Then she went back to the E chart.

"All right," she said. "Now each time I point to one of the *E*'s, I want you

me the direction it's facing. Are you ready,
Junie B.?"

I shrugged again. Then I hid one eye
behind the cup. And Mrs. Weller pointed at
the first *E*.

I pointed my finger up. "That one is facing up at the ceiling," I told her.

"Good," she said. "Excellent."

I felt a little better inside.

Mrs. Weller pointed to the next *E*.

I turned my finger down at the floor. "That one is facing down," I said.

Mrs. Weller smiled and nodded.

I stood up taller. 'Cause this wasn't as hard as I thought.

After that, the nurse kept on pointing at more *E*'s. And I kept on telling her which way they were facing.

"Right . . . left . . . down . . . left . . . up . . ."

I stopped and grinned. "Hey, what do you know? I'm a breeze at this game. Right, Mrs. Weller? Right? Right?" I said.

Mrs. Weller winked at me.

"We're almost done," she said. "Only a few more *E*'s to go."

She pointed to a new row.

There was a fuzzy smudgie next to her finger.

"Whoops," I said. "What happened there? Did someone spill something on your chart?"

Mrs. Weller did a little frown. She kept pointing at the smudgie.

"Can you tell me anything about this mark at all, Junie B.?" she asked.

"Yes," I said. "It's a smearball."

Mrs. Weller moved her finger over a little bit.

"What about this mark here? Can you tell me anything about this one?"

I stared and stared at that thing.

"Hmm. That one's a toughie," I said.

Finally, Mrs. Weller came over to me.

"That's fine," she said. "You did just fine, Junie B."

After that, we played the same game with my other eye.

And guess what?

I saw three more smudgies and a smeary.

After I was done, I sat down in the chair again.

Mrs. Weller said I need glasses.

I do not like Mrs. Weller.

7
Good Guessing

The nurse called Mother at her work.

She tattletaled about the glasses.

Then Mother tattletaled to Daddy. And those two would not let the matter drop.

They talked about glasses all during dinner that entire night.

I couldn't even digest my food that good. Because they kept talking about those stupid, dumb glasses.

"Sooner or later, almost everyone ends up wearing glasses, Junie B.," said Daddy. "Really. They *do*."

I put my chin in my hands real glum.

"Really. They don't," I grumped.

"Daddy's telling you the truth, Junie B.," said Mother. "And besides, you're going to look absolutely adorable in glasses."

"No, I am absolutely not," I grumped again.

"Sure you are," said Daddy. "And just think how great it will be to see the words on the board."

I covered my ears.

"*Not* great, *not* great, *not* great," I said.

Mother took my hands away.

"Listen to me, honey. *Please*," she said. "Glasses are like magic windows for the eyes. When you put them on . . . poof! . . . the whole world becomes crystal clear."

I did a huffy breath.

"Poof, yourself," I grumped.

After that, Mother picked me up.

And she carried me to my room.

'Cause that was one grump too many.

The next morning, Daddy took me to the eye doctor.

The eye doctor did lots more eye tests with me. They were sort of fun. Only I didn't tell Daddy.

Also, the doctor put drops in my eyes. Drops make your eyeballs get biggish and darkish.

Eyeballs look very attractive that way.

After the eye doctor, I went home till my drops wore off.

Then Daddy drove me to school.

And guess what?

All of the children stared at me when I came in the room.

'Cause I was a *late kid,* that's why.

I walked to my desk kind of shy.

Herb's face smiled when he saw me.

"Junie B. Jones! Where *were* you?" he said. "I saved your seat on the bus. But you never came."

"We were afraid you might be sick," said José.

"Yeah," said Lennie. "You're *not,* are you?"

"I certainly *hope* she's not sick," said May. "You shouldn't come to school sick, Junie Jones. Coming to school sick is how germs get started."

I sucked in my cheeks at that girl.

"I'm not *sick,* May. I'm just *late,* and that's all."

May made a grouchy face.

"Well, being *late* isn't good, either," she

said. "Being late gets you a black mark on your permanent record."

I covered up my ears at her.

"Blah, blah, blah, May," I said.

Herb and Lennie and José laughed out loud.

Those guys are starting to enjoy me, I think.

Pretty soon, I took out my workbook. And I tried to do my math.

Only too bad for me. 'Cause I kept on worrying about my new glasses.

What if I look dumb and silly in those things? I thought. *What if Room One laughs their head off at me? What if I look like a goonie bird and no one wants to be my friend?*

The worrying would not go out of my head.

Maybe I needed to talk to someone about this, possibly.

Finally, I reached out and I tapped on Herb.

"Psst. Herbert," I whispered real soft. "I have something I need to tell you. Only I am really afraid to say it. 'Cause what if you laugh at me? Only you probably won't. But I still don't think I should take the chance. And so please do not ask me more about this. And I mean it."

After that, I waited and waited.

But Herb did not ask me.

I tapped on him again.

"Okay. Fine. I'll give you a hint," I said. "But first you're going to have to turn around and sneak a peek at me."

Herb turned around and sneaked a peek.

I quick made round circles with my

fingers. And I held them in front of my eyes.

"Okay, what am I doing here, Herb?" I whispered again. "Huh? What does this look like to you? I'm making round circles in front of my eyes, see? What do you think they are?"

May leaned over to my desk.

"Shush!" she said. "Stop bothering Herb, Junie Jones! If you don't shush right now, I'm going to tell the teacher."

Suddenly, I jumped right up from my chair.

'Cause I *had* it with that girl, that's why!

"NO! *YOU* SHUSH, YOU SHUSHY-HEAD MAY!" I said. "I AM NOT EVEN BOTHERING HERBERT! I AM GIVING HIM A HINT ABOUT MY NEW

63

GLASSES! AND THAT IS NONE OF YOUR BEESWAX, SISTER!"

May's face looked shocked at me.

Her mouth came all the way open.

"You're getting *glasses*?" she said real loud.

"You're getting *glasses*?" said Herb.

"You're getting *glasses*?" said all of Room One.

The children stared and stared.

My head felt hottish and sweatish.

I sat back down in my chair.

Then I looked at Herb kind of sickish.

And I whispered the words *good guess*.

8
Showing-and-Telling

Friday

Dear first-grade journal,

Today I brought my new glasses to school.

They are hiding in my sweater pocket. 'Cause I don't want to put them on, that's why.

My ~~stomick~~ stomach is in a knotball.

Also, there is tension in my head.

We are having Show-and-Tell soon.
I wish this day was over.
From,
Junie B., First Grader

Mr. Scary clapped his hands.

"Okay, boys and girls. Please put your journals away now. I'll give you more time later if you need it. But right now, we have to get started with Show-and-Tell. Who would like to go first this morning?"

May sprang out of her chair.

"I would! I would!" she called out.

Then she quick grabbed a brown envelope out of her backpack. And she ran to the front of the room.

"It's my report card from kindergarten, everyone!" she said real thrilled. "I brought my report card to share with you!"

May waved it all around in the air.

"Look! Look! Can everyone see this? I got all E pluses! E is for *Excellent*! See? There's an E plus next to every single subject!"

She held the report card in front of her. "Okay. Now I will read you each subject one by one," she said.

After that, she took a deep breath. And she started to read.

"Number one: I followed directions.

"Number two: I used my time wisely.

"Number three: I observed school rules.

"Number four: I cleaned up my work area.

"Number five: I—"

Mr. Scary stood up.

"Thank you, May," he said. "That is very interesting. But I'm afraid that we're going to have to move along now and—"

May raised her voice.

"NUMBER FIVE: I WAS COURTEOUS AND RESPECTFUL.

"NUMBER SIX: I USED MATERIALS WISELY!

"NUMBER SEVEN: I—"

Just then, Mr. Scary took May's arm. And he led her back to her seat.

Lennie raised his hand to go next.

He passed around his new styling gel. Plus also, he let us touch his hair.

After that, Sheldon showed us how long he could stand on one foot.

And José sang a song about frogs.

And Shirley showed us her turkey

sandwich. She showed us the bread and the mayonnaise and the tomato.

Finally, Mr. Scary stood up again.

"All rightie, Shirley. Excellent sandwich," he said. "But I really think it should go back in its bag now."

Shirley sat down.

Mr. Scary looked around the room.

"Okay. Who wants to go next?" he said.

My stomach flipped and flopped.

'Cause a nervous idea popped into my head, that's why.

I looked down at my glasses in my sweater pocket.

Then I swallowed very hard. And I quick raised my hand in the air.

"Me!" I blurted out. "I do!"

Mr. Scary smiled. "Great, Junie B.," he said. "Did you bring something to share?"

I quick pulled my hand down again.

"No," I said. "I just changed my mind."

My heart was thumping and pumping.

I peeked at my glasses one more time.

Then all of a sudden, my legs stood up. And they rushed me to the front of the room!

My knees were wobbly and shaking.

I bent over and did deep breaths.

Mr. Scary came over to me.

"Are you okay, Junie B.?" he asked. "Would you like to sit down and wait to do this another day?"

"No," I said. "I want to get this over with."

Then, fast as anything, I reached into my pocket. And I pulled out my new glasses.

May started to laugh.

It was loudish and meanish.

"LOOK! IT'S HER *GLASSES*!" she yelled. "SHE BROUGHT HER GLASSES FOR SHOW-AND-TELL! AND HA! THEY'RE *PURPLE*!"

Tears came into my eyes.

I quick covered my face with my hands. I wanted to sit down real bad. But my legs would not even move.

I stood there very frozen.

And then—all of a sudden—I heard a noise!

It was the sound of running feet, I think!

I looked up.

My new friend Herb was hurrying to the front of the room!

And guess what?

He took the glasses right out of my hand. And he put them on his own face!

"Cool!" he said. "Purple glasses!"

He looked all around.

"Wow," he said. "My eyes could *never* see out of these, Junie B. Your eyes must be really special."

He looked admiring of me.

"How do your eyes even do that, huh? Do you have X-ray vision or something?" he asked.

I shrugged my shoulders kind of shy.

"I don't actually know, Herbert," I said. *"Possibly."*

Herb gave the glasses back to me.

"Here," he said. "Put them on and read something."

I rocked back and forth on my feet.

"Well, okay, Herb. If you insist," I said.

After that, I put on my glasses. And I walked all the way to the back of the room.

I read the announcement off the board.

"Friday, September 23," I read. "Today, get ready for Show-and-Tell."

I smiled real proud.

"The end," I said.

After that, I went back to my desk.

Herb hurried over to me.

He gave me a high five.

And guess what else?

Lennie and José gave me high fives, too!

Mr. Scary did a thumbs-up. "*Excellent* glasses, Junie B. Jones," he said.

"Sí," said José. "Excelente!"

"Yes," called Lucille. "I like those glasses, too, Junie B. 'Cause purple is a popular fashion color this fall."

My heart felt cheery at that news.

I looked at May very smuggy.

"Well, yay for purple," I said.

After Show-and-Tell was over, Mr. Scary gave us more time for our journals.

I picked up my pencil real happy. And I added two more lines.

P.S. Hey! What do you know?
I think I might like first grade!

I looked around the room and grinned.

Everything was crystal clear.

Laugh yourself silly with

ALL the Junie B. Jones books!

Don't miss this next book about my **fun** in **first grade!**

Hurray, hurray! Junie B. is getting to be a professional lunch maker in the cafeteria! Will she be the best lunch lady ever?

Available Now!

Read these other great books by Barbara Park!

MA! There's Nothing to Do Here!

OPERATION: DUMP the CHUMP

Skinny-bones

ALMOST STARRING Skinnybones

THE KID IN THE Red Jacket

GEEK

MAXIE, ROSIE, & EARL— PARTNERS IN GRIME

GEEK

ROSIE SWANSON: FOURTH-GRADE GEEK FOR PRESIDENT

GEEK

DEAR GOD, HELP!!! LOVE EARL

MY MOTHER GOT MARRIED (and other disasters)

DON'T MAKE ME SMILE

The Graduation of JAKE MOON

ALADDIN FICTION

MICK HARTE WAS HERE

Junie B. has a lot to say . . .

the baby's room
Mother and Daddy fixed up a room for the new baby. It's called a nursery. Except I don't know why. Because a baby isn't a nurse, of course.
• from *Junie B. Jones and a Little Monkey Business*

school words
After that, the mop got removed from us. *Removed* is the school word for snatched right out of our hands.
• from *Junie B. Jones and Her Big Fat Mouth*

rules
Me and Mother had a little talk. It was called—*no screaming back off, clown.* Only I never even heard of that rule before.
• from *Junie B. Jones and the Yucky Blucky Fruitcake*

her baby brother
His name is Ollie. I love him a real lot. Except I wish he didn't live at my actual house.
• from *Junie B. Jones and That Meanie Jim's Birthday*

saving a seat
Saving a seat is when you zoom on the bus. And you hurry up and sit down. And then you quick put your feet on the seat next to you. After that, you keep on screaming the word "SAVED! SAVED! SAVED!" And no one even sits next to you. 'Cause who wants to sit next to a screamer? That's what I would like to know.
• from *Junie B. Jones Loves Handsome Warren*

twirling
I twirled and twirled all over the kitchen. Only too bad for me. 'Cause I accidentally twirled into the refrigerator and the stove and the dishwasher.
• from *Junie B. Jones Is a Beauty Shop Guy*

cribs
A crib is a bed with bars on the side of it. It's kind of like a cage at the zoo. Except with a crib, you can put your hand through the bars. And the baby won't pull you in and kill you.
• from *Junie B. Jones and a Little Monkey Business*

... in Barbara Park's
Junie B. Jones books!

ideas
Just then, I smiled real big. 'Cause a great idea popped in my head, that's why! It came right out of thin hair!
• from *Junie B. Jones Is a Party Animal*

punishment
Grounded, young lady is when I have to stay on my own ground. Plus also, I can go on the rug.
• from *Junie B. Jones Is Not a Crook*

apologies
A 'pology is the words *I'm sorry.* Except for you don't actually have to mean it. 'Cause nobody can even tell the difference.
• from *Junie B. Jones and Some Sneaky Peeky Spying*

school
Kindergarten is where you go to meet new friends and not watch TV.
• from *Junie B. Jones and the Stupid Smelly Bus*

**What do parents,
teachers, and kids
have to say to Barbara Park?
Read on for quotes from
real Junie B. Jones readers!**

Here's what parents have to say to Barbara Park:

"My second-grade son has never been all that interested in reading. He came home one day asking if I have ever read about Junie B. Jones. I bought a set of Junie B. books, and now I walk past his room and he is reading on his own!"—*Nancy G., Indiana*

"I have a six-year-old daughter who was fighting us on learning to read. One day, I heard her teacher reading a Junie B. story. We went to our library and checked out every Junie B. book they had. Now we go through one every three days!"—*Sandra L., Idaho*

"Our family wanted to tell you how much we enjoyed your Junie B. Jones books. Our son brought one home from school and we read it together. We all laughed through the whole book."—*Idaho family*

"My daughter and I love Junie B. Jones. She had some difficult times reading in second grade. Your books really helped her have fun while she reads."
—*Barbara M., New Jersey*

"I would like to let you know how much pleasure your books have given us. After my older daughter finishes them, I read them to my six-year-old. You give this world such a gift with your books."—*Amy D., Florida*

Here's what teachers have to say to Barbara Park:

"I've been teaching for twenty-nine years. My class has never enjoyed story time as much [as when I started reading Junie B. Jones]. The class enjoyed her not-so-perfect grammar. We used her sentences for our daily oral language lesson."—*Angie T., Pennsylvania*

"In my experience, students no matter what their age have enjoyed your Junie B. books. Whenever the day is particularly hectic, I can rely on a Junie B. time-out for a relaxing laugh and a reminder to look on the lighter side. You have saved my sanity more times than you can ever know!"—*Shelley M., Maryland*

"Your books have made even my most reluctant readers look forward to each new chapter."
—*Mary Ann O., Illinois*

"Junie B. has touched the hearts of all my students throughout the year. She has become a part of our school lives . . . and in a way, another member of our class."—*Amy P., New Jersey*

"I've been a teacher for more than thirty years and just discovered Junie B. Jones. I noticed that the children have an increased enthusiasm for reading as a direct result of your books."—*Rona G., Maryland*

Here's what kids have to say to Barbara Park:

"I cannot tell you how much I love reading your books! My mom and I laugh so hard, our stomachs hurt and we get tears in our eyes!"—*Kristi O., Pennsylvania*

"I love Junie B. Jones! Every time I go anywhere in the car, I bring at least five Junie B. Jones books. I can't leave home without them."—*Liz O., New Jersey*

"I love your books! You are a very talented writer."
—*Nicole G., California*

"Your books are so cool. You write your books so they relate to life."—*Kayla O., Pennsylvania*

"I love Junie B. Jones books. I think they are *so* funny I could read them all day and laugh out loud. But in the afternoon, I want to watch *Arthur*."—*Laura P., Iowa*

"I love your books so much whenever I'm in bed I always shout, 'Mom! Where are my Junie B. Jones books?!'"—*Tim K., Pennsylvania*

"You write the best books in the world."
—*Manuel L., Colorado*

Raising
Stable Kids
in an
Unstable
World

A Physician's Guide
to Dealing with
Childhood
Stress

DAVID RYAN MARKS, M.D.

Health Communications, Inc.
Deerfield Beach, Florida

www.hci-online.com
www.chickensoup.com

3

Library of Congress Cataloging-in-Publication Data

Marks, David R.
   Raising stable kids in an unstable world : a physician's guide to dealing
with childhood stress / David Marks.
      p.   cm.
   Includes bibliographical references.
   ISBN 1-55874-951-9 (tradepaper)
   1. Stress management for children. 2. Stress in children—Prevention.
3. Burn out (psychology) 4. Children—Mental health. I. Title.

RJ47 .M2575 2002
155.4'18—dc21

                                                      2002023685

©2002 David Ryan Marks
ISBN 1-55874-951-9 (trade paper)

Publisher: Health Communications, Inc.
            3201 S.W. 15th Street
            Deerfield Beach, FL 33442-8190

Cover design by Lawna Patterson Oldfield
Inside book design by Dawn Von Strolley Grove

he said. "Just until you get your bus friend back, I mean."

I tapped on my chin very thinking.

Then, all of a sudden, I raised my voice real loud.

"Why, *sure* you can sit here, Herbert," I said. "You can sit here *forever* if you want to! Because I *used* to have a bus friend named Grace! But today I am dropping her like a hot tomato!"

Bobbi Jean Piper peeked over the seat at me.

"You mean *potato*," she teased.

I sprang up again.

"BOBBI JEAN PIPER WEARS A DIAPER!" I hollered.

Mr. Woo frowned in the mirror.

"Sit *down*, Junie B.!" he grouched.

I sat down.